NELSON CENGAGE Learning™

Australia • Brazil • Japan • Korea • Mexico • Singapore • Spain • United Kingdom • United States

More Like Home

Fast Forward
Emerald Level 25

Text: Carmel Reilly
Illustrations: Christen Stewart
Editor: Cameron Macintosh
Design: Ami Sharpe
Series design: James Lowe
Production controller: Seona Galbally
Audio recordings: Juliet Hill, Picture Start
Spoken by: Matthew King and Abbe Holmes
Reprint: Siew Han Ong

ISBN 978 0 17 012718 9
ISBN 978 0 17 012717 2 (set)

Cengage Learning Australia
Level 7, 80 Dorcas Street
South Melbourne, Victoria Australia 3205
Phone: 1300 790 853

Cengage Learning New Zealand
Unit 4B Rosedale Office Park
331 Rosedale Road, Albany, North Shore NZ 0632
Phone: 0508 635 766

For learning solutions, visit cengage.com.au

Printed in Australia by Ligare Pty Ltd
7 8 9 10 11 12 13 21 20 19 18 17

Evaluated in independent research by staff from the Department of Language, Literacy and Arts Education at the University of Melbourne.

More Like Home
Carmel Reilly & Christen Stewart

IT WAS NIGHT-TIME. FOR SOME REASON, IN THIS TERRIBLE WAR, THE SOLDIERS ALWAYS CAME AT NIGHT. I HAD ONLY BEEN IN A LIGHT SLEEP, SO I WOKE QUICKLY. I HEARD THE SOUND OF SHOUTING, AND THEN GUNSHOTS AND SCREAMS. MY MOTHER CALLED TO ME AND MY BROTHER, *"GRACE, MOSES, GO NOW!"* BUT I DID NOT WANT TO LEAVE WITHOUT HER AND THE BABY. I TRIED TO SAY SOMETHING, AND SHE SHOUTED OVER THE TOP OF THE NOISE. *"WE'LL BE RIGHT BEHIND YOU. JUST GO!"*

MOSES AND I RAN OUT THE DOOR, AROUND THE SIDE OF THE HUT AND INTO THE DARKNESS. BEHIND US, THE VILLAGE GLOWED IN FLAMES. WE RAN AND RAN UNTIL WE WERE COMPLETELY EXHAUSTED. THEN WE STOPPED AND WAITED.

HOW WILL MAMA KNOW WHERE TO COME?
SHE'LL FIND US
BUT HOW LONG CAN WE WAIT?
WHEN THE LIGHT COMES, WE'LL DECIDE.

Running Words 219

MOSES AND I WALKED FOR A LONG TIME. WE DID NOT WANT TO WALK IN THE HEAT OF THE DAY, BUT WE HAD NO CHOICE. WE HAD NO WATER OR SHELTER. THEN, LATE IN THE AFTERNOON, WE CAME TO A VILLAGE.

ARE YOU BY YOURSELVES?
YES.
THE SOLDIERS DESTROYED OUR VILLAGE. WE'RE GOING TO THE BORDER.
THIS IS ALL I CAN GIVE YOU.
IT'S ENOUGH. THANK YOU SO MUCH.
HAVE YOU SEEN ANYONE ELSE FROM OUR VILLAGE?
NO, I HAVEN'T.

HOW FAR IS THE BORDER?
SEE THOSE LOW HILLS THERE? YOU NEED TO CROSS THEM AND THEN WALK FOR ANOTHER HALF DAY. THE REFUGEE CAMP IS ANOTHER DAY'S WALK PAST THAT.
TAKE THESE. IT GETS COLD UP THERE AT NIGHT, EVEN IN THIS WEATHER. BE CAREFUL.
THANK YOU.

I HAD FELT FEAR BEFORE. FEAR HAD BEEN A PART OF MY LIFE EVER SINCE THE SOLDIERS STARTED COMING TO THE VILLAGE. BUT, NOW, I FELT SOMETHING WORSE – A DEEP FEELING OF SADNESS AND LOSS TO BE LEAVING MY HOMELAND.

WE WOKE AT SUNRISE TO THE SOUND OF A TRUCK PULLING UP NEARBY.
QUICK! SOLDIERS!
MY HEART BEAT LIKE A DRUM.
SHH.
WE SAT STILL, HARDLY BREATHING.

DO YOU THINK THEY WERE LOOKING FOR US?

I DON'T KNOW, BUT THEY'D TAKE US ANYWAY. LET'S GO QUICKLY.

THE SOLDIERS OFTEN KIDNAPPED CHILDREN FOR THE ARMY.

I CAN'T SEE ANYTHING, OR ANYONE.

WE JUST HAVE TO KEEP GOING.

THEN, JUST AS I'D ALMOST GIVEN UP HOPE ...
WE'RE LOOKING FOR THE BORDER.
YOU'VE CROSSED THE BORDER. YOU CAN KEEP WALKING WITH US TO THE CAMP. WE'RE ALL GOING TO THE SAME PLACE.
I COULD TELL THESE PEOPLE WERE FROM THE SAME AREA AS US BECAUSE THEY SPOKE THE SAME LANGUAGE.
I LOOKED AROUND, DESPERATE TO FIND A FAMILIAR FACE. FINALLY, I SAW A GIRL I KNEW.
MARIA!
OH! GRACE!
MARIA WAS WALKING TO THE CAMP WITH HER FATHER.

GRACE! MOSES!
WE THOUGHT EVERYONE FROM YOUR VILLAGE WAS DEAD!
WE RAN. WE DON'T KNOW WHAT HAPPENED.
WE CAME PAST YOUR VILLAGE. IT HAD BEEN BURNT TO THE GROUND. IT WAS HORRIBLE. IT DIDN'T LOOK LIKE ANYONE SURVIVED … I'M SO SORRY.

I FELT NUMB AS WE WALKED ALONG THAT DUSTY ROAD. I DON'T KNOW HOW MUCH FARTHER WE WALKED BEFORE THE NIGHT CAME AGAIN. WHEN WE SET UP CAMP, I FELL ASLEEP IN MINUTES.
THE NEXT DAY WE STARTED WALKING AGAIN. MARIA SHARED SOME WATER WITH US. BUT THERE WAS NO FOOD.

WE WALKED FOR MANY HOURS, UNTIL FINALLY ...
IS THAT THE CAMP?
LOOKS LIKE IT.
IT'S SO BIG. IT'S LIKE A CITY OF TENTS.
YOU'LL NEED TO FIND A RELATIVE OR SOMEONE WHO CAN PROTECT YOU. COME BACK TO ME IF YOU CAN'T FIND SOMEONE.
THANK YOU.

ALL THESE PEOPLE.
BUT NO ONE WE KNOW – NO ONE WHO CARES.
WE KNEW WE HAD TO FIND MARIA AND HER FATHER AGAIN. BUT THAT WOULD HAVE TO WAIT UNTIL THE MORNING.
MAYBE MAMA GOT AWAY. MAYBE SHE'S LOOKING FOR US NOW.
MAYBE.

WE WERE LUCKY TO FIND MARIA AND HER FATHER. THEY LOOKED AFTER US FOR THE NEXT FEW MONTHS. AFTERWARDS, MY UNCLE AND AUNT ARRIVED AT THE CAMP AND WE JOINED THEIR FAMILY. BUT, EVEN WITH THEIR HELP AND PROTECTION, LIFE IN THE CAMP WAS HARD. IT WAS OVERCROWDED, AND THERE WERE LOTS OF GANGS WHO FOUGHT EACH OTHER AND STOLE ANYTHING THEY COULD FROM THE REST OF US.

WE WAITED FOR MORE THAN THREE YEARS, HOPING TO BE ALLOWED TO MIGRATE TO ANOTHER COUNTRY – A PEACEFUL COUNTRY WHERE THERE WAS NO WAR.

THEN, ONE DAY, MY UNCLE CALLED US INTO OUR SHACK.

THE JOURNEY WAS A LONG ONE. FIRST WE WENT TO THE CITY. THEN, WE HAD TO GO ON THE PLANE.
IT LOOKS LIKE A GIANT BIRD.
I CAN'T BELIEVE WE'R
FLYING TO AUSTRALIA
I'M SO SAD AND SO EXCITED, ALL AT ONCE.
THIS IS THE START OF OUR NEW LIFE.

THERE'S MARIA!
WELCOME! WELCOME!

THE NEXT MORNING ...
YOU CAN STAY HERE UNTIL WE FIND YOU YOUR OWN HOUSE.
YOU MEAN WE'LL HAVE A PLACE ALL TO OURSELVES?
IT'S SO STRANGE HERE.
YES, IT IS STRANGE.
WE'RE SO FAR FROM HOME.

THERE ARE GOOD THINGS AND BAD THINGS ABOUT BEING HERE, AND SOMETIMES IT'S HARD. BUT MOSTLY, IT'S JUST … DIFFERENT. YOU JUST HAVE TO GET USED TO IT.
THIS FOOD IS DIFFERENT.
I THINK I'LL GET USED TO IT!

I HAVE BEEN HERE FOR TWO YEARS, BUT STILL I MISS MY OWN COUNTRY. I MISS MY FAMILY AND MY VILLAGE. I MISS THE COUNTRYSIDE AND THE TREES AND THE COLOUR OF THE SKY, AND THE SMELL OF THE AFRICAN EARTH. MARIA WAS RIGHT, SOMETIMES IT'S HARD, BUT IT'S GETTING EASIER. WITH EACH NEW DAY, IT'S STARTING TO FEEL MORE LIKE HOME.